JACK MARLOWE

TRULY TERRIBLE TALES

EXPLORERS

h

Hodder Children's Books

a division of Hodder Headline plc

First published in 1997 by Hodder Children's Books

Designed by Don Martin

10 9 8 7 6 5 4 3 2 1

A catalogue record for this book is available from the British Library.

ISBN 0 340 66721 4

Hodder Children's Books
A division of Hodder Headline plc
338 Euston Road
London
NW1 3BH

Printed and bound by Mackays of Chatham plc, Chatham, Kent

Contents

Also in this series

TRULY TERRIBLE TALES

Writers
Inventors
Scientists

Introduction

Everyone enjoys exciting stories. Adventure stories of danger and courage and surprise. But the most incredible stories are often the true ones. Real dangers faced by brave people - or very foolish people who didn't know what they were letting themselves in for! Or greedy people who would risk anything to try to make themselves rich. Or proud people

ANTOINETTE LA BRAVE — EXPLORER

IVAN GREEDOV — EXPLORER

GIANFRANCO STUPIDO — EXPLORER

SIR EGLINGTON PROUDFOOT — EXPLORER

who wanted to be remembered forever. People like explorers.

Explorers can be all of these things. Brave or stupid, greedy or proud.

The stories of four of the world's most fascinating explorers are retold here for you to enjoy. The facts behind the story are as true as a history book can make them.

Parts of these stories are strange and terrible. They are truly terrible tales in fact.

PYTHEAS

LIVED AROUND 330 BC

THE GREAT GREEK

The Ancient Greeks were clever people. They knew that the world was round when everyone else thought it was flat. In 240 BC a scientist worked out that if you went all the way round the Earth you would have to travel 24,647 miles. He was only wrong by 240 miles – and that's not the scientist's fault. It's the Earth's fault because it's not a perfect ball shape.

Of course the Greeks also had some pretty strange ideas. They sailed round the Mediterranean Sea in their galleys and they knew that outside the Mediterranean was the great Atlantic Ocean. But the powerful Carthaginians refused to let anyone sail into the Atlantic. Some Greek writers said that no one could sail the Atlantic anyway – it was too wild and stormy. They believed the legend of Heracles and Atlantis...

The hero Heracles sailed the length of the Mediterranean Sea defeating every monster and every danger that stood in his way. At last he arrived at the western end and found his way blocked by rocks.

Nothing could stop a hero like Heracles. He tore the rocks apart with his mighty hands and made a passage through. A passage through to the Western Sea – the sea we call The Atlantic Ocean.

At each side of the passage he built a mountain of rock and these are the Pillars of Heracles – on a map they are now called the Straits of Gibraltar.

Greek sailors believed the old story that no human can sail on the Western Sea. An old story said that ninety thousand years ago a mighty island stood in that sea. The island of Atlantis. But the people were proud and wicked. The gods could stand it no more and Poseidon, the god of the sea, made the ocean swallow Atlantis and its evil in a single day.

Into the unknown

No wonder the Greeks were afraid to sail into the Atlantic. It needed a brave and determined man to face those dangers. The first Greek to do it was a geographer called Pytheas.

Pytheas took his ship into the unknown. We don't know exactly why he went, but he was probably just desperately curious to know what was out there.

Pytheas wrote down all he had seen and discovered so the Greek people would understand the world they lived in. A copy of his writing would have been kept in the great library at Alexandria – they say every book in the world was there at one time. Then, 950 years after Pytheas wrote his book, Alexandria was

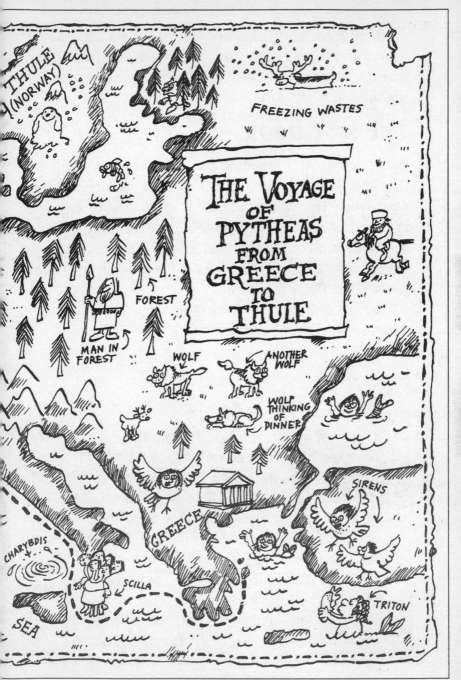

THULE (NORWAY)

FREEZING WASTES

THE VOYAGE OF PYTHEAS FROM GREECE TO THULE

FOREST

MAN IN FOREST

WOLF

ANOTHER WOLF

WOLF THINKING OF DINNER

SIRENS

GREECE

CHARYBDIS

SCILLA

TRITON

SEA

5

captured by a Moslem army. They thought the books were great – great fuel to heat their bath water! Six months later the last book was burned... and I suppose the Moslems had to make do with cold baths!

The lost book

So no copy of Pytheas's book exists. But another Greek called Polybius read the book before it was destroyed. He wrote about it and made fun of Pytheas's story. (He had done a little exploring himself and was probably jealous of Pytheas's great adventure).We have Polybius's book – so we can guess what Pytheas wrote!

The record of his incredible journey into the Atlantic may have read something like this...

DAY 12

The men are afraid. For the last twelve days we have sailed from Massalia [Marseilles in the south of France]. The men were fearless and happy. Sometimes a wind filled our sails and sometimes they rowed. They are used to this. But today we have reached the Pillars of Heracles and the men are talking about the evils that lie beyond.

"Poseidon swallowed Atlantis," Demeter the ship's captain argued. "If Poseidon can do that to a huge island, what will he do to our little ship? He'll swallow us too!"

"I doubt if he'd like the taste of you," I told him. "He'll probably spit you out!"

Demeter grumbled, "But Pytheas, no man has sailed the Western Sea and lived!"

That's when I told him of a curious tale I'd heard back in Massalia. "A sailor from Carthage called Himilico sailed the Western Sea all the way to northern Gaul!"

"I'd like to meet him," Demeter said.

"He's dead," I said.

"Hah!" Demeter cried. "I told you no one has sailed the Western Sea and lived!"

I sighed, "Demeter. Himilico sailed the Western Sea three hundred years ago! Of course he's dead! Many sailors of Carthage sail through and back safely. They spread the stories of the perils because they don't want us Greeks to follow."

The captain sniffed. "It's dangerous and pointless."

"Think of the knowledge we'll gain," I told him.

"Knowledge is no good to a drowned man."

"Think of the wealth we will see in the Tin Islands [Britain]," I whispered.

His face brightened. He looked down the galley and cried, "Right, you cowardly rats. We are sailing though the Pillars of

Heracles to glory!" He winked at me and said quietly, "And to riches, eh?"

Riches do not interest me. I simply want to see what no Greek has ever seen before.

DAY 45

The men are sick. The waves in this Western Sea are as tall as the Pillars of Heracles themselves. They pick up our vessel and drop it like a stone. The men say their stomachs are left up in the sky when they plunge down.

Then there are powerful currents that drag us towards the rocks on the shore. And a strange rush of water to shore every day. I've heard the men of Carthage call these surges of water "tides". I have timed them and I believe they have something to do with the power of the Moon. I don't know how that's possible.

We have no charts to follow, only the Pole Star. We try to stay in sight of the coast but it disappears under a heavy mist of freezing rain. The men are colder than they've ever known.

Demeter is grumbling as usual and some of the men swear they have seen sea monsters ten times as long as the ship. Sometimes, when the mist swirls around us, I almost believe them.

If the weather clears tomorrow we will try to land at one of the villages we see along the coast. Perhaps we can trade some of our wine or olives or honey for some warmer clothes.

DAY 63

Today we reached Belerium [Land's End, England] and it has saved my life. When we landed on the coast of Gaul for fresh water we met sailors who told us about the Tin Islands. They told us they sail out of sight of land for ten days with the Pole Star on their right. That way they come to the tin mines on the Tin Islands.

For ten days we sailed and every day the men became more restless. After eleven days the men wanted to turn around. Demeter stopped them. After twelve days they decided I was a devil and was leading them to Hades [Hell]. It was my fault they were lost in the Western Sea. What's more, I did no work on the ship but sat and wrote this log. They decided it would be best for everyone if they simply turned back... and threw me overboard!

Demeter shrugged and he agreed. The rat-hearted sea-worm was going to let his men murder me! I stood on the highest deck of the ship and tried to reason with them. They shouted and jeered and began to march towards me. That's when I sighted a small fishing ship. "Look!" I cried. "It's too small to stray far from shore! We must be near the Tin Isles. Throw me overboard and your luck will change for the worse."

The men muttered unhappily but returned to their oars. They followed the little fishing boat back to its rough wooden harbour. We saw the Tin Isles and we saw the trading ships loading with the tin.

Suddenly Demeter is not so popular!

DAY 644

We have been travelling round the Tin Isles for more than a year. Some of the men have found land to plant crops that will keep us through the winter and some have stayed on the coast to fish and repair the ship.

I have gone from village to village in the Tin Isles and tried to find out about the natives.

They are really quite simple people compared to the Greeks. They are friendly enough to strangers but quite savage towards each other when they quarrel. In Greece we have great cities. The Tin Isle people have no cities and live in villages under their lord. But some of their customs are quite strange.

I have seen them lay a dead lord in a cart and bury him along with the cart. They take the wheels off and lay them beside the lord. "The lord will use this to travel into the afterlife," they say. "But he must put the cart back together again before he can make it work!"

A dead old horse is placed in the grave and I suppose the poor man must wake that up to pull him along.

The Tin Isle people bury their lord with his armour and his weapons – perhaps he

will meet monsters in the afterlife – and I saw them place half a cooked pig in the grave too in case he gets hungry on his journey, I suppose. I have no idea what the dead horse is supposed to eat!

The people rarely see their lord but live in fear of their priests – they call them Druids. These men train for twenty years and learn to chew dog's flesh so they can see into the future. It seems that they chew the flesh and get the wisdom of the dog! I never knew dogs were so clever!

And their religion is quite dreadful. While our gods live in splendour on Mount Olympus, the people here believe there are gods in trees, gods in streams and even gods in stones.

It is said they make human sacrifices to their gods though I have never seen this myself. But I have seen human heads hanging over the doors of a warrior's hut. The warrior says he gains all his enemy's wisdom and strength. I did not like the way he looked at my wise head!

The people of this island are quite backward. They will never be a great race like the Greeks.

DAY 1231

Now I have reached the end of the world.

I name this place Thule. We can go no further. Tomorrow we turn and go back.

When we had spent three years in the Tin Isles we set sail again and headed towards the Pole Star. We sailed past floating islands made of pure ice. There are wonderful sights here.

In summer the nights are just three hours long. The people here tell me it is because we are close to the home of the sun himself. This is where the sun rests his head every night. The cold here is so great a man's breath turns to ice in his beard. I wish I knew why the sun can keep his light but not his heat when he takes himself to bed.

Here there is no longer land and sea and air – only a cold white wetness all around us and beneath us. Under our feet there is a mixture of ice and water that we slip over and sink into. The ground is like cold jellyfish.

"This is Hades," Demeter told me. He has lived with the Tin Isle people too long. They believe that hell is a place of ice.

Demeter has traded as we travelled. When we return to Greece he will be a rich man. But while he has gathered riches of the world, I have gathered riches of the mind. I have gathered knowledge.

Today we set off home. Today I begin to turn this log into my book called About the Ocean.

When I write my book I shall give the Tin Islands the name that its natives use.

I shall call the little island with the simple people... Britain.

Monster myths

We know many of the Greek stories about gods, heroes and monsters. A poet called Homer wrote a long poem about a sailor called Odysseus who wandered the oceans for ten years. Odysseus had to sail through terror and danger to reach home.

Pytheas and his men would all know the story. But we don't know how many people actually believed those stories. In modern Britain there are many stories about aliens visiting Earth in their Unidentified Flying Objects. A survey showed that about half of the people in Britain believe in UFOs. Perhaps the Greeks were the same.

If the sailors on Pytheas's ship did believe in the old legends then they were very brave men to sail beyond the Pillars of Heracles. They must have expected to meet some of the most terrifying creatures in the world. Which of these sea dangers would worry you?

Gruesome Gods

Poseidon is the king of the ocean. He is a giant who carries a spear with three points – a trident. He uses this spear to stir up storms, to shatter rocks and to create earthquakes. Poseidon's horses have brass hooves and golden manes. They take Poseidon's chariot from his golden palace under the sea. As they ride over the ocean it becomes calm and even sea monsters become tame. Sailors pray that Poseidon keeps the sea just as calm and monster-free for them. Upset Poseidon and you are in trouble! Odysseus poked the eye out of the giant Cyclops to escape. But the Cyclops was Poseidon's son and the angry sea god gave Odysseus a terrible trip home. Do not go around poking the eyes out of strange giants if you want an easy life at sea.

Mischievous Mermaids

The god Nerus, the Old Man of the Sea, is much nicer than Poseidon... though he must look odd with his seaweed hair! He can see into the future. If you capture one of his 50 mermaid daughters then they must tell you the secrets of your future. Very useful ... but a bit of a fishy tale. The trouble is a sailor can easily fall in love with a mermaid. She will persuade him to join her in her home beneath the water and he will drown. Of course, if she tells you your future, you won't be stupid enough to join her, will you?

Come down and see us sometime!

MUSICAL MONSTERS

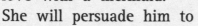

I really like his backing group!

Triton is a fish below the waist – a sort of merman. He makes the roaring sound of the sea by blowing on a huge conch shell. When a human challenged Triton to a shell-blowing contest the mer-man dragged the human under the waves and drowned him. So don't play sea-shells on the sea shore! Another group of pop singers are the sirens – birds with the heads of women. Their songs are so wonderful you have to sail towards them... and wreck your ship on the rocks around their island. (They are the world's oldest rock singers.)

ROTTEN ROCKS

Talking of rocks, there are some pretty cunning ones out there. The hero Jason had to lead his crew of Argonauts between two huge rocks in order to enter the Euxine Sea. The trouble is these rotten rocks, called the Symplegades, have a nasty habit of clashing together as soon as something tries to pass between them. Crunch –

splatt! The Symplegades are not very bright though and Jason found a way to trick them. He released a dove that flew between the rocks. They clashed together. Crunch – splatt! Pigeon pie! Then they opened again.

Yah! Missed!

As soon as they opened, Jason sailed through. So remember – always sail with a dove on board, but don't get too fond of it. Better a dead dove than a battered boat.

▼▼▼▼▼▼▼▼▼▼▼▼ M AN-EATING MONSTERS ▲▲▲▲▲▲▲▲▲▲

Scylla was a beautiful girl... until an enemy fed her magic herbs. Beautiful Scylla grew into a monster with twelve dangling feet, six long necks and heads, and three rows of teeth in each head. Every time a ship sails past her in the Straits of Messina, she feeds each head with an unlucky sailor – that's six sailors per ship. Of course sensible sailors keep well away from her nasty necks. The trouble is there is a huge whirlpool at the other side of the Straits. The whirlpool called Charybdis is so powerful it sucks the entire ocean in three times a day. It sucks little ships in and drowns everyone. It may be better just to let Scylla have her six sailors!

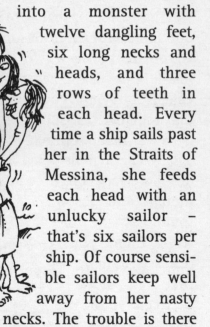

20

Back home

Pytheas returned safely after six years' travel. He was the first Greek to visit the British Isles, the first to write about its people and the first to name it Britain. He was wrong when he said the natives were backward people. They were different from the Greeks, but not stupid. Many explorers seem to make that mistake – they come across native people in a new land and think they are simple minded because they don't speak their language or don't eat the same food.

Just jealous?

If Pytheas expected fame and respect for his work he must have been sad and shocked. Another explorer and writer, Polybius, called him a liar! Polybius had sailed through the Pillars of Heracles but had not made a wonderful six-year journey to the Arctic Circle as Pytheas had. Maybe Polybius was just jealous.

We know Pytheas visited Britain but no one is quite sure where "Thule" may have been. The land of cold white fog and slush could have been Iceland or Norway.

We can't be sure how far Pytheas went. We can be sure that he was an incredible man to sail so far and discover so much. Isn't it sad that his book *About the Ocean* didn't survive?

MARCO POLO

1254 – 1324

THE CHEAT OF CHINA?

Marco Polo was an amazing man. He was either the greatest explorer in the world... or he was the biggest liar in the world!

In 1298 he was captain of a warship from Venice when he went into battle with the fleet from Genoa. Marco's navy lost and he was taken prisoner. But he wasn't thrown into some filthy prison with the common sailors. He was in a more comfortable room and was allowed to talk to the other prisoners. As Marco Polo talked he told wonderful tales. The guards gathered around to listen. The rich folk of Genoa got to hear of the strange prisoner and they turned up to listen too.

Did he tell these stories because he was bored and wanted to pass the time? Or did he tell the stories because they were fantastic but true?

Another prisoner, Rusticello, was a story writer and he wrote Marco's marvellous tales down. When Marco Polo was released two years later the stories were published in a book called *A Description of the World*. It described part of the world his readers had never seen – China.

He told the story of how he met the greatest emperor in the world, a mighty lord called Kublai Khan. And he told truly terrible tales of those faraway places...

Marco's tales

The tale of the Wise Men and the Foolish Caliph

Sit down and I'll tell you all about my wonderful adventures. I'll tell you about my journey to the fabulous land of China. Yes, I've been there and seen it with my own eyes.

My father and my uncle travelled to China when I was a baby. When they returned I was seventeen years old. In a short time they set off for China again, but this time they took me with them. And what adventures I had before I reached China!

Did you know that I have visited Mount Ararat where Noah's Ark landed? It's true, my friends.

And, of course, you've heard of the Three Wise Men? You know, the ones who visited the baby Jesus in the stable. They brought him gifts of gold and frankincense and myrrh. Well, I've seen the three wise men! Of course they weren't alive. They died twelve hundred years ago but I have been to their tomb and seen their bodies.

I had just left the fabulous city of Baghdad. Baghdad was the city of the mighty Caliphs until 40 years ago. The last Caliph was so greedy he hoarded all his gold in a tower and spent nothing on soldiers to defend the city. When Hulagu invaded he took the city easily and locked the Caliph in his tower with all the gold... but no food. Hulagu told him to eat his gold if he could. This was to teach the Caliph a lesson. We'll never know if he learned the lesson because he starved to death!

There is another story that the Caliph was wrapped in a fine robe, thrown on the ground and trampled to death by stampeding horses. I can believe either. The people of that region are cruel and wicked.

But, as I was saying, I passed Baghdad and reached the city of Saba in Persia. That's

I could do with a dash of salt.

where the Three Wise Men came from. I was taken to a cool dark tomb and shown their bodies. Only skeletons now, of course, but they still had their beards and hair. A wonderful sight and I am the only man in Europe to have seen it!

Marco probably saw the remains of some old kings. But were they the Three Wise men of the Bible story? We'll probably never know.

Marco also repeated stories he'd heard about the lands he passed through. Some sound truly terrifying!

The tale of the hot wind and the Assassins

We left Persia and the Three Wise Men and set off on the most dangerous part of our journey. The journey across a great desert. Even the cities on the edge of the desert were like ovens.

You think it gets hot here in Genoa in Summer? You should go to Hormuz on the

Sorry, market's closed until noon.

Persian Gulf. We passed Baghdad and went to Hormuz to trade in spices, pearls and cloth of gold. The markets sold fine ivory from tusks of giant elephants. But they never trade from nine in the morning till noon when the hot wind blows. Instead they go to the river and stand up to their necks in the water.

This wind is called a "simoon" and they tell a story of his terrible power. They say that an army marched to attack Hormuz but the attackers were caught by the hot wind. It suffocated every single man. When the people of Hormuz went to bury them, the bodies crumbled and turned to dust and blew away.

We left Hormuz and its fearsome heat and we went into the desert with only lakes of poisoned green water. Finally we came to the city of Tunocain. That is the home of a band of murderous men they called "assassins". These men were devoted to their leader who was called "The Old Man of the Mountain." Whatever the old man ordered them to do they would obey. He sent them out to murder a Shah of Persia, a Grand Vizier of Egypt and some of our greatest knights who led the Christian Crusades. The Old Man's assassins were so devoted to their leader they would die for him. They say two young men stood on top of the highest tower in

Damascus. When the Old Man gave the word they threw themselves off to a dreadful death. Of course he promised them a place in heaven if they died for him. That's why they took so many risks.

The mighty Hulagu destroyed the Old Man and his Assassins just as he'd destroyed the Caliphs of Baghdad. And so we survived to travel East to China.

The Assassins really did exist. But do you believe that story of a wind that can turn an army to dust?

The story of the rat-eating men and the wolf-killing women

When we'd crossed that terrible desert we reached the country of Mongolia.

That's where the fierce Mongol Tribes live. They shelter in tents that are the shape of bee hives and when they move they carry them on carts pulled by more than twenty bullocks. But they are most famous for their horses which they can ride two days and nights without stopping.

The Mongolians eat everything including dogs and rats. They also eat horse flesh and drink the milk of mares. They even drink the

fresh blood of their horses in winter to keep warm then the Mongolians close the wound and ride on. To cross a river their travellers rope their horses together and cling to them as the horses swim to the other side.

The Mongolian women are as hard as the men. I was shocked to see they wear trousers and boots like a man and ride as well. I have seen a woman shoot a wolf and even go with her man to war. They say that washing clothes in a river would upset the god of the river. So they never wash their clothes.

These fierce Mongolian fighters defeated the Chinese. The people of China are much cleaner. Their important leaders take a holiday every tenth day to have a bath.

The strange Mongolians are so different. Their priests take the shoulder bones of sheep and roast them in a fire. They take them out and look at the cracks. This, they say, tells them what will happen in the future.

Yet the leader of these wild Mongolian people is a great and peaceful man, Kublai

Khan. When we arrived at his court he looked at me and said, "Who is this young man?"

My father told him and Kublai Khan said, "He is welcome and he pleases me much."

He gave me wealth and power. I was just over twenty years old when he made me governor of the city of Yangzhou.

Great story! The trouble is the city of Yangzhou has a list of all of its governors. Historians can look at it today. The name of Marco Polo is not on that list. Oh dear.

The story of the siege of Sa-yan-fu and the thunderbolts

I was the most popular governor that the city of Yangzhou ever had. I spent many happy years there. But the time came when I had to leave it to fight for the emperor Kublai Khan.

From time to time he had trouble with some of the cities in his empire.

Let me tell you about the time when my father and I won a war for the emperor Kublai Khan. It was at the city of Sa-yan-fu in China. The people of Sa-yan-fu had refused to obey the emperor and for three years they had shut the gates of the city while his armies surrounded it.

My father and I knew about weapons we had seen back home in Italy. Giant catapults that could fire boulders big enough to crush a house. We call them mangonels. We showed the Mongol generals how to build three of these weapons and we watched them rain boulders down on Sa-yan-fu.

The people of Sa-yan-fu believed they were thunderbolts from heaven. They gave up immediately. The brains of the Polo family had won when the might of the Mongol army had failed. We were heroes!

The emperor said he would grant us any wish. We asked if we could return home to Venice to see our old friends. Emperor Kublai Khan was disappointed but he granted our request. And so 1 returned.

1 was the trusted servant of the greatest emperor in the world and now 1 am a prisoner in Genoa.

But one day 1 will be free. One day the world will read the adventures of the great Marco Polo!

Another great story! Chinese history shows that Sa-yan-fu was defeated in 1273... but Marco Polo didn't arrive in China until 1275! Oooops!

The travels of Marco Polo

Marco was released in 1299 and his book was published. It was read by thousands of people. Two hundred years later a sailor read it and decided to find a way to get to China without crossing deserts and facing all the dangers.

The sailor decided to go west, across the seas and round the world till he reached China. The sailor's name was Christopher Columbus... and he never reached China. He came across another land that even Marco Polo didn't know about. Christopher Columbus discovered America.

What Marco said...

Marco Polo reported meetings with strange people and creatures as he crossed the world.

He wasn't the only one to bring back truly terrible tales of monsters. Which of these creatures would you like to meet? People in the Middle Ages believed these things all lived in distant lands...

You look like a dog's dinner!

Cannibals who had human bodies but the heads of dogs! (A merchant told Marco Polo he'd seen these in the Andaman Islands east of India. Imagine that! You would be dog food to them!)

Birds called rocs that were so huge they could swoop down and pick up an elephant. They would drop the elephant from a great height so it would burst open. Then they'd eat it! (Another of Marco's reports. You'll be pleased to hear these birds only live in Africa.)

Ooh, I'm terrified of heights!

A fish that was sixty metres long and covered in hair. Marco said he'd actually seen the head of this monster but the 60-metre body had already been eaten. (This sort of creature could supply your school with fish fingers for years.)

A headless giant with his face on his chest and a one-legged giant who could lie on his back and use his huge foot as a sunshade. (To be honest, Marco never mentioned these weird creatures. But a publisher put pictures of the giants in Marco's book and Marco was blamed for inventing them.)

No wonder people in Venice called Marco Polo a liar. His friends back home begged him to change his stories and tell the truth. He told them he'd actually seen more incredible things than these.

The trouble is, poor Marco also told many true stories and no one believed him.

Ask an adult

Find an adult. Test their brain power with these questions. Here are seven things that Marco Polo described. Many people in Venice called him a liar.

Marco, like Pytheas, said there was a land where it is always night in the winter and always daylight in the summer. People laughed at him but we know such a land does exist north of the Arctic Circle

Now we know the following six things really exist. But what are they?

A nut that was as large as a man's head and covered in hair. People of Venice laughed because they had never seen such a thing. You have. What is it called?

A cloth that couldn't catch fire – people of Venice refused to believe it. What was the cloth made from?

3 Black stones that burned longer and hotter than wood – the people of Venice shook their heads in disbelief. What do we call the black stones?

4 Human beings who lived in the trees and used their tails to balance or hang from branches. People of Venice gasped. What were these monster men?

5 Huge serpents with legs. They lived in the water but could crawl out and snap up a human in one bite of their giant jaws. What do we call them?

6 Pictures that appeared in the air as you crossed the desert. When you walked towards the pictures they vanished. What would modern travellers call them?

What Marco didn't say...

Marco Polo sometimes told true stories and sometimes it seems that he lied.

But there is a story even stranger than Marco's terrifying tales. Some historians believe Marco Polo never went to China at all!

In his book Marco never mentions some very important things. For example, the emperor Kublai Khan built a great observatory so his scientists could study the stars. It was a famous building but Marco never says a word about this in his book. It makes you wonder if he really went to China at all. There are other important things missed out. Things like...

❖ *Tea* Everyone in China drank tea but Marco never mentions it though he said he spent seventeen years there. Strange.

❖ *Printing and books* The Chinese used printed paper money, which Marco mentions – but he doesn't say that it was made by printing with wood blocks. The Chinese also printed books and sold them at markets. Odd.

❖ *Chinese writing* – very different to the writing in Marco's Europe. Perhaps he couldn't read. Weird.

❖ *Chopsticks* They always ate with chopsticks, but maybe Marco didn't notice. Peculiar.

❖ *Foot binding* Chinese women had their toes curled under their feet and bound. Marco says the women were beautiful and described their jewels but forgets to say how they were cruelly forced to hobble around. He doesn't mention the fashion for long fingernails either. Curious.

❖ **The Great Wall of China** – a wall so big it can be seen from outer space. Marco must have been blind to miss this 30,000-mile monster. Incredible!

Fantastic fibber?

You might believe that Marco Polo never went to China. His book said he did – but Chinese books of the time don't say anything about Kublai Khan's great friend from Venice. In Chinese history the famous Marco Polo is never mentioned once.

When he returned home the people of Venice didn't seem to believe him. And they should know. There was a story about the return of Marco and his father. It says they stepped ashore in Venice after 17 years in China. They were dressed in Mongol clothes and no one remembered who they were. The Polos had almost forgotten how to speak Italian.

But the travellers then split the seams of the ragged and travel-worn clothes... and out tumbled diamonds and pearls, rubies, sapphires and emeralds. All the riches they had earned in China.

That sounds a wonderful tale but it's almost certainly not true. The Polos did not live like rich men when they came back to Venice. A rich man would

not have gone out fighting against Genoa... and if a rich Marco had been captured he would have used his riches to buy his freedom. He would not have spent two years trying to write a book!

Marco – the truth?

So, if Marco didn't go to China, how did he come to write that book?

Perhaps Marco had just read some old travellers' books and listened to stories of people who really had been to China. His own father and his uncle almost certainly met a Mongol prince and returned home with stories. Maybe Marco turned the stories into a script when he was trapped in prison and because he wanted to make himself some money.

Even if he wasn't a great explorer, his book was important. After all, a sailor called Christopher Columbus believed it. And look at the great discovery that led to. The discovery of America!

Sir Walter Raleigh

1554 – 1618

THE HEADLESS HERO

The Tudor age was one of the great times for exploration. Greek explorers like Pytheas had been trying to discover more about the world they lived in. Middle Ages explorers like Marco Polo were looking for trade. But the Tudors had different reasons for sailing the seas. They wanted the fabulous wealth they believed was on the far side of the world... and they wanted to stop their enemies from getting it first!

The Tudors were not bothered that this wealth belonged to someone else – the native peoples of the countries they explored. They thought they had the right to go to another land, conquer the people, steal their wealth and carry it back to Europe. Truly terrible Tudors!

In Tudor times England's greatest enemy was Spain. The countries argued about religion and they argued about who should sit on the throne of England. But most of all they argued about the New World, America, and all its wealth. Spain sent explorers to bring American gold and silver back to their king. England sent explorers to steal the Spanish treasure from under their noses.

Of course such ruthless explorers often came to a truly terrible end. Men like Walter Raleigh – who suffered the terror of being beheaded... twice!

If the Tudor and Stuart people had newspapers then Sir Walter would have made headlines. Headlines like these, perhaps...

WALTER'S WONDERFUL VIRGINIA VENTURE

Sir Walt presenting Her Maj with some spuds at the palace yesterday.

Sir Walter Raleigh, the dashing young adventurer, has claimed a large slice of America for England... without even setting foot on the place!

Young Walt made a name for himself fighting for his Queen and country in Ireland. He had the nerve to tell Queen Bess just where the battling Brits were going wrong. Queen Bess likes a man with bottle and he soon became her favourite. She gave him vast amounts of land in Ireland, licenses to trade in wine and cloth, and made him admiral of Devon and Cornwall. In 1587 Sir Walt became captain of the Queen's Guard and the gossips were saying there'd be

continued from page 1
wedding bells within a year or so. Jealous rivals nicknamed him King Walter but couldn't do much to stop the Queen adoring him.

The Queen even admired the riches he brought back from America – not gold but a strange vegetable called patata by the natives. Some cooks say you can boil it, mash it, fry it, roast it or bake it. Envious enemies say it will never catch on in England.

Now wily Walt has crossed the Atlantic and explored the east coast of north America. He claimed it for England and named it Virginia in honour of Queen Bess, known as the Virgin Queen. Sir Walt sent an expedition of 100 men and 17 women to build a colony on Roanoke Island. The colonists have just celebrated the birth of first English child ever to be born in the New World. Naturally she was called "Virginia" – just as well it wasn't a boy! His real plan is to have the whole continent, north and south America, as English colonies.

When Sir Walter Raleigh thinks, he thinks big!

A right royal welcome for baby Virginia!

48

Bessie's Blue-eyed Boy in Bother!

Sir Walter Raleigh, the favourite man in Queen Elizabeth's life, is in prison! His crime? He married the wrong Elizabeth!

Sir Walter seems to have blown his chances of becoming King – and maybe his chances of keeping that handsome head attached to his shoulders! He met Elizabeth Throckmorton five years ago and some people say he married her back in 1588. Elizabeth Throckmorton was one of the Queen's own maids of honour. Crafty Walt kept the marriage secret from jealous Queen Bess. But when she found out how he'd lied for four years she threw Walt and wife in the Tower of London. It doesn't pay to cross a queen and Walt may suffer a pain in the neck. A very sharp pain!

Some of his enemies were laughing till the tears ran down their ruffs. Walt must be a worried man as he looks out through those narrow windows of his cell.

Sir Walter: "The world itself is but a large prison, out of which some are daily led to execution".

Don't talk to me about potatoes!

WOE FOR WEARY WALTER

Dreams turned to dust today when Sir Walter Raleigh returned to England empty handed. The Queen's former favourite set off to South America to find the legendary city of Eldorado – the city of Gold. In 1592 he was imprisoned by the Queen but used some of the money from a pirate expedition to buy his freedom.

Good Queen Bess released him – but never really forgave him.

Walt decided to get back into favour with the greatest exploration ever. A trip that would bring back enough gold to make her majesty the world's richest woman. Walter had read Spanish documents that told the tale of Eldorado. On his last trip

High hopes – Walt gets water-borne, heading for El Dorado.

"Weedy" Sir Walter puffing tobago.

he'd heard stories from the natives about the golden city. He set off to find the dazzling legend.

The brave Englishman sailed up the Orinoco River through the very heart of Spanish territory. But all he found were a few gold mines – and no one willing to stay and explore further.

Sir Walter arrived home yesterday and took his gloomy report to the queen. She is said to be very disappointed.

Walt is of course famous for sucking at the smoke from a dried weed. It is called tobago by the natives and Walt picked up the habit when he was in America. Many men at Elizabeth's court are copying this disgusting habit. They call it "smoking". Raleigh will have to come up with something better than burning weeds if he wants to win Queen Bess's heart. Stick that in your pipe and smoke it Walter!

51

Jim's jolly joke rattles Raleigh

Sir Walter Raleigh got the shock of his life yesterday ... and nearly went off his head with worry. Or, rather, his head nearly went off him! Our new king, James, had caught the rotter Raleigh plotting to throw him off his throne. Raleigh was arrested and sentenced to death. Being a knight Raleigh would have the honour of being beheaded ... a commoner would have been hanged.

The plotters were a feeble group and good King Jim pardoned them one by one. But there was no pardon for wicked Walter. On the morning of the execution the ex-explorer was led out to the block and told to say his last prayers. As his head rested on the block a messenger galloped into the castle with the king's pardon. Joking James had deliberately left it till the last minute!

Sir Walter was recovering in the Tower last night with his family. They will all spend the rest of their lives there.

Friends report that Wally did not see the funny side of King Jim's jest!

Of course it is well known that King James hates the disgusting habit of smoking and Sir Walter smokes like a wet wood fire!

11 NOVEMBER 1616

WALTER GOING FOR GOLD!

Adventurer, sailor, writer and traitor, Sir Walter Raleigh, is free after 13 years in the Tower. He is to lead a new expedition to South America to find the great golden city of Eldorado. James agreed to release Raleigh when the man promised to return with untold riches.

The king has made it quite clear that he does not want problems with our friends in Spain. Things have changed since Sir Walter went into the Tower and war with Spain is just not on.

The old explorer will take his son with him on the expedition.

POTATO MAN HAS HAD HIS CHIPS!

Sir Walter Raleigh, the man who brought the first potato to Britain, has finally lost his head. He was executed today for the treason he committed 15 years ago!

Two years ago he set off to find Eldorado but King James ordered that he must not upset the Spanish. Unfortunately he fell ill with a fever when he reached South America. His son and one of his Captains set off to find Eldorado. They disobeyed orders and attacked a Spanish settlement. Sir Walter's son was killed and the Spanish survivors were furious. In order to keep the peace with Spain, King James had to agree to execute Raleigh when he returned.

Fifteen years ago Sir Walter Raleigh was par-doned. This time there was no last minute let off. He knew he was finally facing death and went to the scaffold with a joke. A servant offered to comb his ruffled hair; Sir Walter said, "Let the people who get my head comb my hair!"

He spent his last night writing a poem which ended,

And from the earth and grave and dust
The Lord shall raise me up, I trust.

Sir Walter ate a good breakfast and smoked a final pipe full of tobacco.

Sir Walter wore black as he limped to the scaffold – his leg had been injured in the Battle of Cadiz against the Spanish. He turned to the executioner and said,

54

"Show me your axe." Then he tested the blade and said, "This gives me no fear. It is sharp and a good medicine to cure me of all my diseases."

The executioner took off his cloak and spread it on the ground for Sir Walter to kneel on. This reminded people of the old story – it was said that Sir Walter had spread his cloak over a puddle so Queen Elizabeth would not wet her feet.

The old man knelt down and said, "When I spread my hands, execute me." He spread his hands. The executioner waited. Sir Walter looked up and cried, "What are you afraid of? Strike, man, strike." The axe fell.

As one of the watching crowd said, "There was not another head in England like this."

Cruel conquests

The trouble with explorers is they are not always happy to visit a place then go home the way Pytheas or Marco Polo did. The Tudor explorers tried to settle in some of the new lands they discovered. This often led to disaster for the settlers and for the natives.

Sir Walter Raleigh knew this. He wrote:

> The miseries of war are great when a nation leaves its own land and roots out the natives of another land to make room for itself. The attackers take little with them; they must take everything from the natives – land, cattle, homes and even the cradles of the babies. These merciless wars are the cruellest of all.

Raleigh saw all this in Ireland with his own half-brother Sir Humphrey Gilbert – but it didn't stop him leading invasions. There are many truly terrible tales of suffering settlers and their nastiness to natives. Here are just ten...

Merciless massacres

In 1569, Sir Humphrey Gilbert went to Ireland to bring peace. The starving peasants were fighting against the English rulers. Sir Humphrey Gilbert's idea of "peace" was a vicious one. If a town surrendered then he would spare the people. But if a town tried to fight him then he would massacre everyone inside it – including the babies. Every night when he

made camp he ordered his men to cut the heads off the bodies of the people killed in the fighting. He lined the road to his tent with these heads. Any Irish man or woman wanting to speak to him had to walk along that gruesome trail, fall to their knees and beg for mercy. At first Sir Walter seemed to think these terrible methods worked. Later he changed his mind – maybe he was sickened by the massacres he had taken part in.

Death by squirrel

In 1583 the grisly Gilbert sailed the Atlantic and tried to set up a colony in the place we call Newfoundland. But the colonists rebelled and he was forced to return home. Sir Humphrey could have sailed in his leading ship, The Golden Hind. Instead he chose to sail in the little frigate The Squirrel, just a quarter of the size of The Golden Hind. When the ships hit a storm it was the little Squirrel that sank. Sir Humphrey Gilbert drowned. In 1611 the great explorer Henry Hudson also had trouble with rebel crew in his expedition. They put him in an open rowing boat with his teenage son and set him adrift. Since they were in the Arctic at the time he was certain to die a slow and cold death.

Disappearing islanders

Sir Walter Raleigh sent settlers to make a new life for themselves on Roanoke Island in 1587. Three years later a map-maker called John White went to take them supplies. There was not a single living person on Roanoke Island. There was just one clue as to how they had disappeared. Someone had carved the word "Croatan" on a tree. Croatan was a nearby island. Did the settlers cross to Croatan and live with the friendly native Americans there? No one knows for sure. It's one of the great mysteries of history.

Poor Pocahontas

In 1606 an English soldier called John Smith went back to Virginia and tried again to set up a colony of English people. The settlers suffered disease and starvation as well as attacks from native Americans. Smith was captured and about to be executed. A 10 year-old girl rushed forward, laid her head on Smith's and pleaded for his life. (Her head was bald because that was the fashion in her tribe at the time!) Smith was spared and left with the little bald girl – her name was Pocahontas. But there was no happy ending. The English gave Pocahontas a new name – Rebecca – then they gave her a trip to London. Finally they gave her the disease, small pox, which killed her. The settlers that John Smith left behind were almost wiped out by the Indians.

Sacrificed to slavery

The Spanish conquered islands in the Caribbean and land in South America. They killed warriors who stood in their way and turned many others into slaves. The natives died early from overwork or disease. The British sailor John Hawkins discovered that the Spanish wanted still more slaves so he collected 300 from Africa and transported them across to America where he sold them for a good profit. When Elizabeth I heard of this she saw it as a good way of making money. In 1564 she gave Hawkins a loan to buy more slaves and make another trip. This time she shared in the profit. There were 250,000 natives on Hispaniola when Christopher Columbus arrived. Slavery killed off almost 200,000 of them.

 Nasty natives?

Christopher Columbus was the first European to find America in 1492. But seven years later an explorer from Florence followed and wrote a book of his adventures. The explorer was called Amerigo Vespucci and the new continent was named after him – America – and not after Columbus. Amerigo wrote terrifying tales of the natives he met. The stories were so horrible the explorers who followed took powerful armies and were keen to destroy those natives. Amerigo Vespucci wrote, "They have no laws and no religion, no king and no one to rule them. They are brutal people who pierce their lips and cheeks with bones to make themselves look fierce. In war they kill without mercy. They bury the bodies of their friends but they cut up and eat the dead bodies of their enemies. The live enemies are made into slaves and sometimes offered as human sacrifices and eaten."

 ## A treacherous trap

The truth is the invaders were as cruel as the natives. In 1532 a Spanish invader called Pizzaro didn't mind cheating a bit. He invited the leader of the Incas in Peru to meet him in a fortress. The Inca leader, Atahualpa, agreed... and walked straight into a deadly trap. He was handed a Christian prayer book but threw it to the ground. That was a signal for Pizzaro's men to attack. They were hiding around three sides of the fort – they blasted Atahualpa's men with cannon fire and then charged at them on horse. Pizzaro's 150 soldiers killed 3,000 of Atahualpa's Indians and captured him. Greedy Pizzaro asked for a ransom of half a million pounds of gold before he would release the Inca chief. The Incas paid the ransom ... then Pizzaro executed Atahualpa anyway!

 ## An extraordinary escape?

The explorers from Europe didn't always win. In 1527 an expedition set out to explore the jungles to the north of Mexico. No one heard of them again until

1536. Then just 4 men turned up in Mexico City and said they were the only survivors of the 80 who had set out nine years before. The men said Indians had captured the whole expedition and turned them into slaves. After six years these four had escaped. They worked their way back from the jungle, pretending to be doctors and curing sick Indians. Some people who heard their story said their escape was a miracle – others said they were fakes. It's another mystery of history.

A vile voyage

In 1520 the first man to try to sail around the world was Ferdinand Magellan of Portugal. He never made it... but a tiny part of his expedition did. Five ships set out – one returned. 265 men set out – only fifteen lived to tell the terrible tale. Some of the sailors tried to mutiny and they were hanged. Some died of starvation and others survived by eating leather sail-covers, sawdust and rats. Magellan reached the Philippine Islands in 1521 and agreed to help a tribal chief in a battle against another tribe. He lost and was killed. His crew survived and sailed on led by navigator Sebastian del Cano. Magellan is remembered because his name was given to the channel at the southern tip of America. Del Cano is almost forgotten!

10 Diehard Drake

Sir Francis Drake was the first English captain to lead an expedition around the world. But, like Sir Walter Raleigh, he had to be a ruthless man. A gentleman on board his ship became the leader of a group of grumblers. Drake invented a crime and had the gentleman executed. He returned and was welcomed as an English hero by Queen Elizabeth. He helped the English defeat the Spanish Armada before finally dying of a fever. He was buried at sea. Now a legend says that Drake is just sleeping. When England is in danger from a foreign invader he will rise from his ocean grave and defend the country. Britain survived World War II and German U-boat attacks without

Drake waking up... at least no one reported the appearance of a dripping skeleton leading the attack!

Fascinating fact Christopher Columbus set out to find Marco Polo's Spice Islands by sailing west. He knew he had to sail half way round the world to get there. When he'd sailed about 6000 miles he reached the West Indies and thought he'd found the Spice Islands. This was because he thought the world was about 12 000 miles around and he really was half way round it!

Christopher Columbus never believed he'd discovered a new continent to the day he died. As a result the new continent, America, was not named after him!

Yet Pytheas and his Greek friends knew that the world was 25 000 miles round and they lived over 1 800 years before Columbus set sail. If Columbus had read Greek books as well as Marco Polo's book then today's maps might show the "United States of Columbia" instead of the "United States of America".

In fact the Spanish did call America "Columbia" for three hundred years after Christopher's death. The rest of the world didn't agree and the Spanish gave up and started calling it "America" too.

FLORENCE BAKER

1841 – 1916

A NILE NIGHTMARE

For hundreds of years adventurers had been going round the coast of Africa. They said they were "trading" but really they were stealing. Stealing people. They made a huge amount of money from kidnapping African people, cramming them into ships, and carrying them across the Atlantic Ocean. When they arrived in America the lucky Africans were sold as slaves – the unlucky ones died on the journey, of course!

In 1833 the British finally banned slave trading. There was no longer a profit to be made in facing the heat, the disease, the wild animals and the hostile tribes. Yet brave Brits still went back to Africa. This time they went to explore the inside of Africa, not just the coast.

The great River Nile river flowed past the pyramids and out into the Mediterranean Sea. But no one from Europe had ever seen the start of the Nile – its source. That became the explorers' dream of the 1860s... to find the source of the Nile. The first person to find the source would be famous forever, the Victorians believed. And so the race began. The race to be first.

In fact we now know the Nile has two sources. The great Lake Victoria was found by explorer John Speke in 1864. But the second huge lake was found by the most remarkable African explorer of all. A fantastically fabulous female called Florence!

THE
FABULOUS
FLORENCE

"Stepmothers are wicked," Anna said. She's only ten years old and she can't even remember our real mother.

"Who says?" I asked her.

"My book. Hansel and Gretel had a stepmother and look what happened to them!" she cried. My sister was as pale and wide-eyed as a frightened ghost.

The fire crackled in the hearth but the servants hadn't been round to light the gas lamps. Flame-shadows flickered over the dark carpet and the wind rattled the windows. The evening was hurrying in even faster than the wind. In the grey light outside the window the gardener worked in the flower bed.

"Hansel and Gretel's just a story," I told Anna.

"But aren't you scared, James?" she asked me.

"I'm scared of no one and nothing," I said. "When I grow up I'm going to be a great explorer like our father."

"And I'm coming with you," she said eagerly.

"Girls don't often become explorers," I sniffed.

"Our stepmother did," she answered. "That's what makes her so scary! Read me father's letter again."

I sighed. I'd read the letter to her twenty times and it was creased and worn now. I pulled it out of my pocket and read it aloud.

James and Anna, my dearest children,

You will be pleased to know that I am safely back in Cairo and will soon be heading home to you in England. But there is one thing I must tell you before I arrive. I will not be alone. I will have a new wife, a new step-mother for you.

I know you love your dead mother but I am sure you will learn to love Florence in her own way. She is a remarkable woman and I want to tell you just a little about her before you meet her next month.

When Florence was only seven years old, younger than you, Anna, she lost her family. There were lots of rebellions in Eastern Europe that year and Florence's family were caught up in one. She doesn't remember too much about what happened. It was too horrific for a little girl. She will only say, "I have memories of gunshots and the screams, the corpses and fire. I hid in a cupboard to escape and I stayed there a day. When I came out everyone was dead."

A kind family gave her shelter and brought her up as their own daughter. But her terrors weren't over. Within ten years there was another rebellion and this time Florence was captured. She was captured by slavers who put her up for sale in the town of Widdin.

You may remember that I wanted to go to Africa with the explorer Livingstone but he turned me down. So I travelled down the Danube River instead. By some strange

chance I arrived in Widdin just as Florence was being paraded in the market place for sale. I could see that the young woman was terrified. I could see some cruel Turks bidding for her. I knew that they would buy her, work her to an early death then go out and buy another slave to take her place.

So, just as the auctioneer was about to sell her to a bald man with broken yellow teeth and a fist full of golden rings, I put in a higher bid. I think everyone was too shocked to think of bidding more. No one else said anything and Florence was mine.

Of course we don't have slaves in Britain. I said to her at once that she was free to go. The poor woman told me she there was nowhere that she could go. She asked if she could come with me.

As you know, I have always had this mad urge to explore Africa and find the source of the river Nile. I was planning a new expedition and I warned Florence that I'd be leaving for Egypt soon. She said she would like to come with me.

I knew that Africa was no place for a

woman. Not an ordinary woman. But Florence was different. I really believed she could survive in the awful climate and some of the terrors that lurked there – the disease and the wild animals and wilder humans. Florence nearly didn't survive, but then I almost died too.

She never complained and I never regretted taking her. We set off up the Nile and the heat was terrible but she rode on though she was exhausted. She always said the same thing, "Where you go, I go."

And Florence has been a great help keeping records of our journey, making maps and recording everything we saw. Most of all she kept me going. Look at the maps in your school geography books, James. You'll find Gondoroko, a thousand miles up the Nile, then ... nothing! No European had ever been further! It was the edge of the world.

What your map book doesn't show you is what a filthy, dangerous place Gondoroko is. Everyone is involved in the slave trade and everyone carries guns. We had our own workers with us to carry our

equipment – they weren't slaves, of course, we paid them well. But when they got to Gondoroko they wanted more. They wanted me to give them free time so they could go on slave raids of their own. I refused, of course, and forty of them came for me with guns. It was only Florence who could make them listen. She stood between me and my rebellious workers and saved my life. It wasn't the first time or the last!

No sooner had she saved my life than I wished I was dead! Two Europeans came into the town. They were John Speke and James Grant and they told us they had discovered the source of the Nile! It was a huge lake and they had named it Victoria after our Queen. Of course I was heart-broken. I'd wanted the glory of that discovery. What was there left for Florence and me to discover, I wondered?

Then Speke told me about another lake to the west of his Victoria. The natives called it Luta N'Zige – the Dead Locust. It was another source of the river Nile but Speke wasn't able to explore it. A tribe called the Bunyoro lived there and their King Kamrasi refused to let anyone explore it.

I said at once that I'd go there myself and fight this King Kamrasi if I had to. It would be dangerous. Speke and Grant were on their way home and offered to take Florence with them. She refused, of course. So we set off on the most deadly part of the journey. Imagine it, James. A vicious king ahead of us and our workers

ready to shoot us in the back!

The journey itself was miserable enough. There's a fly called the tsetse that was biting the donkeys and camels and killing them. Our workers began to desert us and Florence and I had to take turns staying awake at night. We knew that if we both fell asleep the men would cut our throats, steal our equipment and head back home.

Somehow we reached the Bunyoro king-
dom and got to meet the dreadful King
Kamrasi. I was polite to him, you understand, and asked if we could have his
permission to visit the Dead Locust Lake.

"Of course you can," he said. "If you pay
me."

"I'm a rich man. How much money do
you want?" I asked.

He just shrugged and said money was no
use to him in Bunyoro. Then he pointed to
Florence. "I want your woman slave. I
want a European woman to add to my
collection of wives!"

If I refused then he'd try to make my
journey impossible. If I accepted then
Florence would return to the slavery I'd
saved her from! What would you have
done, Anna? James?

I'll tell you what I decided – though it
almost cost us our lives. I decided we
should go ahead against the wishes of
the King. He was furious. We were
afraid that he might send warriors to
attack us at any time. But we discovered

there was something worse than the fear of enemy warriors. It was worse because it was invisible!

We'd set off across plains covered in bushes and reached swamps that gave off terrible evil air. I have seen some terrible places made by humans but never such a one created by nature. I've seen castles with dungeons as deep and dark as the underworld itself. I have seen slums in the cities of Europe that have turned my stomach with their smell of

death and rottenness. But I've always felt free in the open air. That swamp on the Nile was the most evil place nature ever made.

The air itself made us ill. We weren't used to it! No one from Europe had ever passed that way before or breathed that type of air. Florence and I were the first. It was as we came to a bridge of reeds that Florence first complained she felt faint.

The choking, stinking evil scent of the place was suffocating her. So many things had died and rotted in that swamp. It was like an open graveyard.

I wanted her to go back, but she insisted, "Wherever you go I will follow. Though I walk through the valley of the shadow of death," she said. And death's shadow was on her in that place. We stepped onto the reed bridge and walked over the green and black water. Bubbles of foul-smelling gas were rising to the surface and suffocating me. The bridge was too long for us to hold our breaths all the way across it.

Florence was half way when she says the whole sky seemed to swirl around her and she fell onto the bridge. That strong woman was suddenly too weak to crawl. I watched helpless as she began rolling to the side of the bridge and towards the dark liquid. I grabbed her just as she was about to fall off the edge.

Then there was nothing but darkness and dreams for Florence. It is something your doctors call 'delirium'. Wild, frightening dreams from which you cannot wake.

You had a fever last year, Anna, so you know what I mean.

I swear that anyone else would have died of that fever Florence had. I've always said that death is a coward, James - if you fight him hard enough he will let you live.

But I didn't believe even Florence could cheat death that time. She was in a dead faint for days. I kept the group marching forward to get her out of the swamp. I wanted to make camp on the shores of

Lake Luta N'Zige. If we could only get there the fresh water would help. The porters carried her and I held up her head for miles so she wouldn't choke. At night I dripped water into her mouth so she wouldn't die of thirst.

It was when we reached the hills above the Dead Locust lake that she finally stopped shivering and moaning. She was still and cool and I knew she was all but dead. I ordered the men to start digging her grave. I wanted it deep where the jackals couldn't get at her body.

And then there was something I can only describe as a miracle. One of the workers came running to me and said Florence was awake and asking where I was. Somehow she'd cheated death again.

Anyone else would have wanted to turn around and head home after that. But Florence said, "I have come to see Dead Locust Lake. Let me see it."

We were weak with malaria – both of us – but we struggled up that final hill. Porters said there was a glint of water to be seen from the top. It was hard work getting there and it was harder getting down the other side. The bushes and the grasses were so thick and rich. It took us half a day to cover that last mile.

But it was worth it for we saw the most wonderful sight – a sight that no one from Europe had ever seen before. A mighty lake – one of the two sources of the Nile! The explorer John Speke had called the first lake Victoria after the Queen. Naturally we decided to name this lake Albert – in memory of Victoria's husband.

One day you'll have to go there, James –
perhaps you may want to go too, Anna.
Look at the clear blue waters of Lake
Albert. I even drank the water of the lake
to celebrate. It was the sweetest water
I've ever tasted and it is the sweetest
feeling to be the first man in Europe to
set eyes on it. That's what exploration is
all about, my children.

Florence limped down to the edge of the
water and took her ribbons – the red the
green and the white of Hungary – and
she tied them to a bush on the shore of
Lake Albert.

So you see, my children, why Florence is
so special. We will travel to England a
week after this letter leaves Egypt. We
plan to stop in London for a few days
and get married. But I wanted you to be
the first to know this.

I wanted you to know something about
her before you meet her. She is an extraordinary woman and is desperate to
make a good mother to you, James and
Anna. I can only pray that you will take
her to your hearts.

I folded the letter and put it back in my pocket. "She'll be here soon," I said.

"Imagine exploring Darkest Africa!" Anna said. "She must be monstrous!"

"Who must be monstrous?" the voice from the doorway said.

Anna squawked like a pheasant that's seen a fox. I swung round and saw Florence standing in the doorway. "Good evening, Anna," she said. "Good evening, James."

"Good evening," we croaked in reply. She was tall and looked as strong as our gardener. Her black hair was parted in the centre and pulled back from her high forehead. It was held by red, green and white ribbons. Even though her face was in the shadows of the doorway her dark eyes sparked and burned with life.

"Who must be monstrous?" she asked. Her low voice had a German accent.

"Hansel and Gretel's stepmother," I said quickly. "We were talking about stepmothers."

She smiled and moved slowly into the room. "And you think your new stepmother may be as wicked as that?" She leaned forward and looked at me. "I know dozens of dark forests in Africa. Should I take you out there and leave you?"

Anna gasped.

The woman's dark eyes glinted in the firelight. "Sorry," she said, trying to keep her face straight. "I was teasing, Anna. I promise not to leave you in the forest or make you serve in the kitchens like Cinderella's stepmother. I know what it's like to be a slave."

Anna relaxed and sat on the hearth rug at her feet. I sat on the stool at the far corner of the hearth. "What do we call you, Stepmother?" I asked.

She stared into the flames and frowned. "I think I would like it if you called me Florence," she said finally.

Anna looked up at her shyly. "Is it true you went into Darkest Africa?" she asked.

As Florence opened her mouth to reply she heard a sound from outside the window. Even in the flickering glow of the fire her face turned pale. "What was that noise?" she cried and clutched at her throat.

"The gardener, planting a rosebush by the window," I told her.

Her hand slid down to her chest and pressed against her heart. She looked at me wild eyed and said softly, "Do you know the worst sound in the whole world?"

"A rosebush being planted?" I asked.

She shook her head. "No. It is the sound of a grave being dug... but especially when that grave is your own! I was close to death once," she said. "But something woke me. A sound. It was the harsh scrape of shovels in the hard earth and the thud-thud of the soil being piled up. Somehow I managed to force my eyes open and saw the porters digging a trench. I asked one, 'What are you doing?' He looked at me terrified. 'Digging your grave!' he said... then he ran to fetch your father. Now I can never hear the sound of shovels in the earth without trembling."

Suddenly our new stepmother stood up. "But that's a story for another evening by the fire," she said as she rose to her feet. She walked to the door and stopped. "That is... if you want to live with a wicked stepmother, of course," she said.

Anna grinned at me across the glowing warmth of the fire. "We do."

And as darkness finally swallowed the garden, the gardener picked up his shovel, placed it in his barrow and walked away.

Florence Fact File

Waking to hear her own grave being dug was just one of Florence's amazing adventures. Some of the following incredible things really happened to her – but not all of them! Can you guess which are true and which are false?

1 Florence rode a camel to travel up the banks of the Nile. To do this she did something shocking for a woman in Victorian times... she wore trousers. Some of the natives thought she was Sam Baker's son!

True/false? ◇

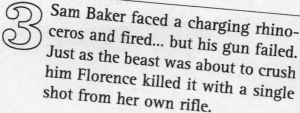

When Sam Baker and Florence reached Africa they woke one night to find a hungry hyena in their tent about to make a meal of them.

True/false? ◇

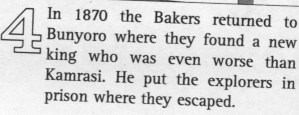

Sam Baker faced a charging rhinoceros and fired... but his gun failed. Just as the beast was about to crush him Florence killed it with a single shot from her own rifle.

True/false? ◇

In 1870 the Bakers returned to Bunyoro where they found a new king who was even worse than Kamrasi. He put the explorers in prison where they escaped.

True/false? ◇

When the Bakers fled from Bunyoro they were chased for seven days till they reached the safety of Gondoroko. Day after day they dodged showers of spears from the king's warriors.

True/false? ◇

Queen Victoria was so delighted with Florence's discoveries that she welcomed her back to Britain with a great party.

True/false? ◇

Thank you so much!

Answers

All are true... except number 6. Queen Victoria should have been thrilled that Florence had helped a Briton to discover an important lake and name it after her husband, Albert. In fact Queen Victoria was a snob and thought it was disgraceful that a woman should wear trousers and go exploring. She refused to meet Florence.

However, the British people loved the explorer and cheered her wherever she went to speak.

Florence returned to Sam's home in England and became very popular with Sam's children whose mother had died several years before.

Florence Baker, who died in 1916, was an amazing woman... and definitely not a wicked stepmother!